ISBN: 978-0-9849588-3-2
Library of Congress Control Number: 2013933411

Edited by Tamurlaine Melby
Design by Tom Trenz

BELLE ISLE BOOKS
www.belleislebooks.com

Dedicated to my mother, Gertrude, who taught me that style begins inside, and to my grandchildren, who continue to teach me that style should bring a smile.

Rainbow was almost four years old.

She loved shoes very much.

She loved pants and shirts.

She loved skirts.

She loved dresses. She especially loved dresses that looked like princess dresses. They were long and poofy and usually had sparkling buttons or flowers or shiny little stars.

Rainbow simply loved clothes.

Now that Rainbow was older, her mother let her help pick out her clothes.

It was the night before Rainbow's first day of school. It was only preschool, but it was still school for Rainbow. She was very excited.

Before bed, Rainbow's mother said, "Now we will pick out your outfit for tomorrow. You should look nice for your first day of school."

Her mother opened the pants drawer in Rainbow's dresser. "Which pants do you want to wear tomorrow?" she asked Rainbow.

Rainbow looked at the pants. She saw purple pants with flowers. She saw orange pants with little red bows. And then she saw her favorite pants.

They were pink and white striped pants with pink flowers around the cuffs that looked almost real. "Oh," said Rainbow smiling, "I want to wear these pants. Okay?"

"Sure," said her mother. "They are very cute."

"Now we must pick a top for you to wear," her mother told her.

They looked in the drawer with tops. Rainbow pulled out a blue shirt with an orange bear on it. "I want to wear this one," she said.

Rainbow's mother looked at the blue shirt and frowned. She said, "Rainbow, how about this white shirt with the pink collar? It would be so cute with your pink and white striped pants."

"No, no, I want to wear the bear. I don't want to wear the white shirt. Please?" she asked nicely.

4

Her mother held up another shirt. "This pink shirt is very pretty. How about it?" she asked.

Rainbow shook her head. She knew she wanted to wear the bear shirt on her first day of school.

Her mother thought to herself that pink and white pants with a blue and orange shirt would not match, but she did not want to hurt Rainbow's feelings. So she just said, "Okay."

5

Rainbow's mother then opened up the sock basket. "Let's get some socks for you to wear."

Rainbow immediately reached into the basket and pulled out some bright green socks. The socks had red polka dots on them. "These. I want these socks, Mommy."

Her mother looked at the bright green socks with red polka dots and said, "Rainbow, you are going to have so many colors with your pants and your shirt and now your socks. Are you sure you don't want to wear these new white socks we bought?"

"No, I want to wear the green socks," replied Rainbow firmly.
"I like them."

Her mother sighed but nodded.

"Okay, now let's get your shoes," her mother said.

Rainbow had three pairs of shoes. She had a black pair that she wore for dress up. She had a pair of brown sandals that used to belong to her friend's brother. And lastly, she had a pair of yellow sneakers with brown laces.

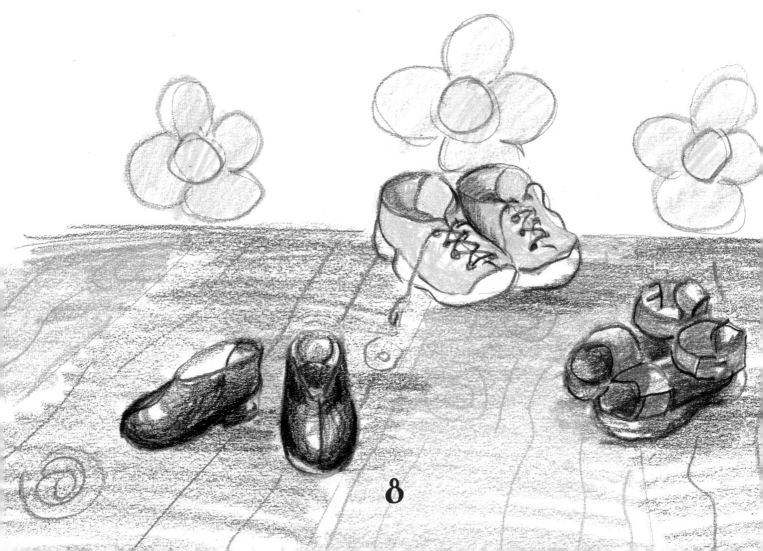

Her mother held up the black shoes and said, "Rainbow, how about these?"

"No," answered Rainbow. "I want to wear the yellow shoes. They are so comfortable."

Rainbow's mother threw her hands up in the air. "Okay," she said. "Yellow shoes it is."

So Rainbow's mother folded up all the clothes Rainbow had chosen and set them aside for the next morning.

That night after Rainbow was in bed, she heard her mother talking to a friend on the phone.

"Rainbow is ready for school. She picked out her own clothes. She will look ridiculous because nothing matches," said her mother.

Rainbow was sad to hear that because she loved everything she had picked. She did not understand what her mother meant. Soon, Rainbow fell asleep.

The next day, Rainbow dressed herself. She was proud when she looked in the mirror. She loved her pink and white striped pants with the pink flowers around the cuffs. She loved her blue shirt with the orange bear on it. She loved her green socks with the red polka dots. And she loved her yellow shoes with the brown laces.

12

She found a barrette with a purple and blue ribbon. She put it in her hair. Rainbow smiled. She thought, "I look great!"

When her mother saw her, she said, "Rainbow, you look … well, you look very colorful."

Rainbow could tell that her mother did not really like the clothes she was wearing. She asked, "Don't you like my outfit? I love it!"

Her mother said, "It's okay. You seem happy."

Rainbow was happy. It was her first day of school. She felt proud of herself when she entered her classroom.

Her mother told her goodbye, and Rainbow found a place to sit.

16

That morning the teacher, Miss Pickit, explained what they would be doing in school. They would talk and read books and draw pictures and pretend different things and take walks outside and even have playtime. Wow! Rainbow liked school already.

Then Miss Pickit told the children, "We are going to talk about some colors. There are so many colors in the world. They are all around us. Let's see who knows their colors. I am going to call out a color, and if you are wearing that color, you can come to the front of the classroom."

First Miss Pickit said, "Brown. Anyone wearing brown, please come to the front of the class, and I will give you a smiley sticker."

Three boys wearing brown shorts walked to the front of the room. Rainbow looked down at her clothes. She wasn't wearing brown shorts like the boys. But then she remembered that her shoelaces were brown, so she left her chair and walked to the front of the class.

"Here you go," Miss Pickit said, and she handed each of them a sticker with a smiling brown bear on it.

Then Miss Pickit said, "Yellow. Anyone wearing yellow, please come forward."

One little girl was wearing a very pretty yellow dress, so she went forward.

Rainbow looked down at her yellow shoes and knew she could go, too.

Miss Pickit gave both girls
yellow smiley face stickers.

21

Then Miss Pickit said, "Pink.
All of you who are wearing pink,
come here."

Rainbow was glad she had pink stripes on her pants. Rainbow and one other girl wearing a pink tee shirt went to the front of the class. "Here you go," Miss Pickit said, and she gave them stickers with smiling pink flowers on them.

Then she said, "Blue." Almost everyone in the class was wearing blue, so Miss Pickit said, "I will walk around and give you all this sticker." It was a blue star with a big smile. As she walked by Rainbow, Miss Pickit told her, "You have a blue shirt and blue in your hair ribbon. You get another sticker."

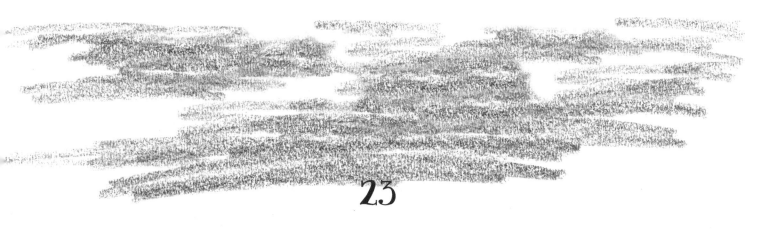

"Okay," said Miss Pickit, "now green. Anyone wearing green, please come here." Five more students got stickers, and so did Rainbow. She was wearing green socks.

Then Miss Pickit called, "Red." Four students went to the front. Rainbow went, too, because her socks had red polka dots. They all got stickers with smiling red hearts.

25

Then Miss Pickit said, "Orange." No one else was
wearing orange. Only Rainbow. She had an orange
bear on her shirt. Miss Pickit gave her a sticker of a
smiling orange pumpkin.

Miss Pickit said, "Rainbow, you have received a sticker each time and now it is time for purple. Are you wearing any purple?"

"Yes I am," said Rainbow, remembering her hair bow was blue and purple. Miss Pickit gave Rainbow another sticker.

Then Miss Pickit said, "Well class, we have talked about a lot of colors today and you have all received prizes for knowing your colors. But I have one more prize to give. This prize will go to the student who wore the most colors today. Does anybody know who that student is?"

All the children answered, "Rainbow!" So Rainbow went to the front of the room. Then Miss Pickit gave her the best prize of all: a beautiful **red** ball with many colored spots on it. There was a **brown** spot and a yellow spot. There was a **pink** spot and a **blue** spot. There was a **green** spot and an **orange** spot and even a **purple** spot. Rainbow took the **red** ball with the many colored spots. She was so happy.

29

That afternoon when Rainbow's mother picked her up from school, Rainbow showed her all her prizes. Rainbow said, "See, I did pick out good clothes. Look at all the smiley stickers I got, and a ball, too!"

Rainbow's mother smiled. It was true. Rainbow was happy with what she wore.

And maybe that was what really mattered.